Best Wishes 💗

Big Hearts

Debbie Wolfe 💗 Olive

The Adventures of OLIVE

and Her Big Heart

The Fire

By Debbie Wolfe

◆ FriesenPress

Suite 300 - 990 Fort St
Victoria, BC, V8V 3K2
Canada

www.friesenpress.com

ISBN
978-1-5255-8764-1 (Hardcover)
978-1-5255-8763-4 (Paperback)
978-1-5255-8765-8 (eBook)

1. JUVENILE FICTION, ANIMALS, DOGS

Distributed to the trade by The Ingram Book Company

This is a story about a doggie
named Olive.

When Olive was a puppy, she was all alone.

Olive chewed on her stick alone.

Olive played with her toy alone.

She sat.

She played.

She walked in the snow alone.

Month after month, Olive's heart was empty.

Just when she couldn't imagine what to do next
- she saw a girl.

They ran to each other and **hugged** and **hugged**.

Olive's new friend **LOVES HER SO MUCH!**

Olive's empty heart filled and grew with **LOVE!**

Every day Olive's Heart
grew **BIGGER** and **BIGGER**.

As Olive grew older, she was so grateful for her new friend's love.

She wished nothing more than to share her **BIG HEART** with others.

And so begins - **The Adventures of OLIVE!**

Olive is an Alaskan Malamute.

She lives in Alaska.

Alaska is a northern state that gets very cold.

Olive talks by sounding "*Woo Woo.*"

Because of this, her other name became **"WooWoo."**

Humans and animals
understand Olive's language.

Olive has a **BIG HEART!**
She is always trying to help.

She wants every creature to
be **safe** and **happy.**

One day Olive was playing on the
beach with her dog friends.

After her friends went home, Olive sat and wondered how she could share her **Big Heart** with others.

Suddenly her friend, Mr. Eagle, flew over and landed.

Mr. Eagle told Olive,
"A terrible fire has started and is spreading out of control!"

Olive worried about all of the humans and animals who could be in danger.

She jumped up and barked, "*woo woo! Woo woo woo!*" asking Mr. Eagle to fly around and find those in danger.

Then Olive ran to her friends at the Fire Station.

She began **"woo wooing"** the news of the fire. The firefighters thanked Olive for alerting them.

Moments later, Mr. Eagle swooped down and told Olive, "Your friends, The Wolf Pups, are in danger!"

Olive understood the situation.

She ran to the helicopter.

She went with the firefighters on the helicopter.

Mr. Eagle led the way.

When they landed, Olive jumped out and found her Wolf pup friends.

She "*Woo Woo'd*" to her Wolf pup friends that it was ok to follow her to the helicopter.

Olive waited until every Wolf pup was on the helicopter.
Then she followed.

They flew off and **ALL WERE SAFE!!**

Flying back to the village, Olive looked down and saw Mrs. Moose acting strangely.

When the helicopter landed, Olive ran to Mrs. Moose.

Mrs. Moose said, "Mamma Bear and her cub are in danger down by the river."

Olive ran as fast as she could.
She came to the big river.

Mamma Bear and her cub were trapped by the deep fast river. The fire was right behind them!

So Olive **"Woo Woo'd"** to her beaver friends. The beavers understood the danger.

The beavers began chewing on the bottoms of the trees with their sharp teeth.

Just as the fire got to
Mamma Bear and her
cub, a tree fell across
the deep fast river.

Mamma Bear and her cub ran on the tree, over the river, to safety.

Olive **"WooWoo'd,"**
"Thank You" to the beavers!

Mamma Bear was so grateful and thanked Olive for her **BIG HEART!!**

ALL WERE SAFE!

THE END

CPSIA information can be obtained
at www.ICGtesting.com
Printed in the USA
BVHW020251190721
612207BV00001B/1